PETROL

Other books by Martina Evans

POETRY

The Iniscarra Bar and Cycle Rest
All Alcoholics Are Charmers
Can Dentists Be Trusted?
Facing the Public

FICTION

Midnight Feast
The Glass Mountain
No Drinking, No Dancing, No Doctors

Martina Evans

Petrol

ANVIL PRESS POETRY

Published in 2012
by Anvil Press Poetry Ltd
Neptune House   70 Royal Hill   London   SE10 8RF
www.anvilpresspoetry.com

This book is published with financial assistance
from Arts Council England

Designed and set in Monotype Bembo by Anvil
Printed and bound in Great Britain
by Hobbs the Printers Ltd

ISBN 978 0 85646 448 5

A catalogue record for this book
is available from the British Library

ACKNOWLEDGEMENTS

Thanks to Arts Council England
and the Royal Literary Fund
for their assistance
– M.E.

for Jane Young

Main characters

JUSTIN	Proprietor of McConnell's bar, shop and petrol station
IMELDA	His thirteen-year-old daughter and the narrator
BERTHA, AGNES	Her older sisters
CLODAGH	Their prospective stepmother
GRANDDAD	Justin's father
DANNY BOY	A nineteen-year-old farmer
NEILY SHEEHAN	Proprietor of the rival JFK bar

'But I don't want to go among mad people,' Alice remarked.

'Oh you can't help that,' said the Cat. 'We're all mad here. I'm mad. You're mad.'

Alice in Wonderland

I

I WAS under the table with the sugar bowl the day of the funeral and I heard the women saying Justin had killed Mammy. But I thought I was the one who killed her. And the spoon was shaped like a small spade and I sucked hard as I listened. *He might as well have put the gun to her head, twenty-nine miscarriages, sure who in the name of god would put up with that?* The women wore thick tan tights and one woman's legs went in a straight line from knee to ankle. *The last one put her clean out of her mind.* The table was shaking, they were buttering the bread so hard and I dipped my spoon in the sugar. Last time Mammy took Agnes and me down the fields, she took all her clothes out of a big suitcase and threw them into the river and started bawling crying. Agnes ran in to save the clothes but I was only thinking of my stomach. I thought we were going on a picnic, where was the lemonade and tomato sandwiches? A horsy headscarf hung from the hawthorn like a flag, Agnes was up to her knees in green weeds and I was examining the welts on my hands where Mammy's ring squeezed too hard. I wished hard that she'd die like Bertha's Mammy and three weeks later she had.

2

FACE your Fears, said Justin, as he backed out of the cat shed. *There's a rat in there. Agnes better get the shovel* and Agnes did and I followed at a distance, thinking of the shopkeeper who pulled a handle sticking up out of a side of ham and wasn't a handle at all, it was a rat and it turned round and bit him to death when he pulled. Our rat was dead of course but Agnes was always brave, with her brown eyes and barley sugar plaits, pulling on the big gloves for dipping the petrol tank. *Why is it always me?* Agnes said and the rat's tail swung at the end of the shovel. *Carrying the weight of this family.* I was behind her in the gloom, always wanting to be that saintly, too. The rat-filled cats lay in the hay, their eyes like stringed lights lighting our sisterly way and *Is it codding me you are?* said Justin when I said I was worried about the snake coming down from Dublin and Agnes and Justin laughed and held their sides as if they were in a Shakespearian play. Justin put a Hamlet cigar in his mouth, told me I would do well to listen to my teachers – hadn't they told me that Saint Patrick had driven the snakes out of Ireland. *But the Zoo*, I said. *But the Zoo*, he repeated in a squeaky voice, mocking me, asking me did I think I was that important out of all the places where an escaped snake might go, interesting places like the hill of Tara or the Rock of Cashel. *Do you mean to tell me that he would turn off the main road just to make his way to your bed? Face your fears.* Justin said it again when he said I wasn't allowed down after eight o'clock. It wasn't that dark with the lights from the cars outside and the glow from the Major Cigarettes sign lighting up the page but sometimes the mice wouldn't stop running inside the panelling and there was the strange smell from the possessed girl's room in *The Exorcist* and having to go to the bathroom and passing Mammy's grotto where the cabbage-green snake was biting the Virgin Mary's foot and I was always afraid Mammy's ghost would appear to me high above the green linoleum stairs.

3

BLOODY *Marys, Jaysus!* Granddad was disgusted beside the range, Lucky standing on his lap, wet nose pointing high in the air when Agnes ran in from the bar, her brown velour arm wrapped around the plastic ball of the Coca-Cola ice bucket. *It's far from ice they were reared!* Granddad said but Justin always made Bloody Marys for his favourites, slim dark women who wore their clothes like Jackie Kennedy. It was a big operation with all the stuff and the Tabasco sauce stirred with a long clanking spoon. Granddad ground his teeth as Agnes tore the tray from the side of the yellow-iced freezer, staggering on her high brown clogs in her modest A-line corduroy skirt. I, too, was thinking she was too good for this work. *They don't know what they want*, Granddad said. *Ice one minute, hot whiskeys the next. Those bloody women.* The Bloody Mary drinkers. And his last comment when the ice cubes tumbled into the Coca-Cola bucket, *every single woman that Justin ever took on suffered from her nerves.*

4

BUT I can't believe Justin would confide in you, Agnes said. *But, you are the one* Justin said under the lilac tree, *you are the one to make Clodagh feel at home with your books and your love of flowers.* I started watering the geraniums and straight away they were pointing their buds at me. They knew I was the one, the only one who could make Clodagh feel at home. Bertha said it was disgrace at his age. I couldn't say that I thought it was desperate romantic with Agnes's brown eyes gone black with rage. She made two vodka and Britvics when Justin was at the Cash and Carry and Consulate smoke billowed above our sipping heads. *But I can't believe he would confide in you.* Agnes couldn't stop saying it and to be honest, I couldn't believe it either. Suddenly I was great – *highly-strung, over-sensitive, dreamy* – all these things were great now. I was the only one who would understand Clodagh and I had his treacle eyes and special attention fixed on me. I basked in the smell of his Hamlet cigars, pretending to know less than I did because Bertha and Agnes were very angry. Bertha said there might be no money left for our education, where did I think the money was going to come for a third wife? *But she's a teacher*, I said. *She has her own money.* — *Oh, that won't last long,* said Bertha. *Hasn't every wife ended up bedridden?* — *But he's had only two,* I said. — *Only two? Only two?* said Bertha. *Isn't one wife enough for most men around here and isn't he about to take a third?*

5

BUT someone might kill Justin. In the bad old days, I wished for this as I wished death on Mammy and Ould Farrell as well, with his watery old eyes and hands like a pair of coal tongs pulling me on to his lap, scraping his stubble on my cheek when I was small. Justin stuck his head over the counter then with a bottle of Time in each hand, saying *caught the two of ye!* Caught the two of ye. What had I done? Ould Farrell was the first one I killed by thinking. A magician came to the national school and clicked his fingers, the very same way Justin did when he said we were sinking into debt from too much eating. I'd be afraid to click my fingers in case the whole world might drop down dead at my feet. But I couldn't get the slitty black magician eyes out of my head. He called me out of my desk to help with a trick. He'd a soft white rope and he said he'd suspend me upside down from the ceiling to show off my figure and everyone laughed the way they laughed in the bar when Justin made a joke against someone.

6

THE voices rose and fell in the bar every night and someone shouted, *Noble call, come on now, noble call.* You had to sing if it was a noble call and shy singers made a big noise clearing their throats first. Everyone liked singing *As I was slowly passing an orphan's home one day* except that Justin said Bat Ahern shouldn't really sing that because he was an orphan and he really *was* nobody's child. Justin said it was too much, Bat rubbing it in like that. It was bad for business. *Oh for god's sake no Mommy's kisses, no Daddy's smile. No, we can't have that here tonight, no way! No flowers growing wild, Bat, for feck's sake.* Justin shouted at Bat that he was putting everyone off their drink and Bat tried to climb over the counter to take Justin by the throat. Justin laughed loudly when he was painting over the scuffmarks the next day, said he'd never been frightened at all and he only blamed himself for serving Bat in the first place because Bat was only looking for trouble. Agnes said that Bat would be back, *sure he secretly adores the ground Justin walks on.* But Bat stepped out of the church on Sunday mornings in his navy suit with his hair oiled and a straight crease in his hair so white, I could see it from the shop window three hundred yards away. He drove away in his Morris Minor with a face like the villain Judd from *Oklahoma*. *Poor Judd is Dead*. I tapped a knell on the bar counter with the knife for flattening the pints of porter. They said Ould Farrell died a bad death but I didn't wish Justin death yet.

7

GRANDDAD had seventeen cats, he ran down the path reunited with them after he was away, crying *I'm back! I'm back!* Justin said the bailiff would be in. All over a pack of unhealthy cats. The waste of food was something savage and you wouldn't hear of it out of tinkers. Anyway, I was on lookout when Justin was busy talking to the men in the bar saying the IRA were completely right and giving out about the Jews and Granddad's tongue was out as he sawed the ham for the cats with a bread knife because the sound of the electric slicer would alert Justin. But Justin was as quiet as a cat himself in his Hush Puppies and he must have gone out the bar door and in the front door because he came silently from the other direction with the exaggerated steps of a stage villain. But the shop door bell rang and Granddad was able to run with the ham and Danny Boy walked in, his blue eyes, like Henry Fonda's, blazing out of his oil-streaked face. His salmon corduroy flares were dusty too, he smelt of diesel and Major cigarettes and Bourneville chocolate and he tore off the chocolate wrapper with his beautiful brown fingers and always offered me half but not today with Justin holding up the mutilated mound of ham and asking us how in the name of god was he going to sell that? Saying that it was only a matter of time before the bailiffs were in and then Justin went quiet and his eyes were as hard as Black Jacks watching me as I added up the messages, *three cans of Batchelors beans, four sliced pans,* holding my breath, *twenty Major and a box of matches.* My cheeks hot enough to melt tar. *That is one pound and twenty-nine new pence,* I said and Danny said I was as good as a ready reckoner and I wished he hadn't said that because Justin said that Danny was very easy to impress and everyone knew that Agnes was the brainy one and Justin didn't take his disgusted eyes off my red face, looked like he'd forgotten all the good things he'd said under the lilac tree. When Danny went out, Justin's voice was just like the electric slicer and he asked me did I know Danny Boy was so stupid the Master put his head through a blackboard years ago.

8

THEN Justin sent Agnes away to relations she didn't know from Adam and she said she knew that he was up to something and she was so mad, she would give the bailiffs something to think about when they came round. Justin was filling up the Mini when she went round the shop, plucked two packets of hair clips off their cards – twang, twang – a cardboard packet of needles in the shape of a basket of flowers, a reel of black cotton, a reel of white cotton and a very old dusty-pink one with the plastic covering gone yellow. She took two Gateaux Swiss Rolls because she said, *If he thinks that I'm going to turn up at the Clohessys' house with my hands hanging to me, he's got another think coming to him.* And she looked right at me, *I have an awful feeling you know something you're not telling me. How would you like if he did that to you? He rang them up, he didn't know them from Adam, never interested in them in his life, then rang them up and asked them to take me! Me, that he can't manage without for five minutes.* The petrol pump hummed when Agnes wrapped a bottle of Hennessey in her Southern Comfort sweatshirt. Justin replaced the nozzle, opened the car bonnet and poured water from a Pyrex jug into the radiator.

Agnes was kneeling by her duffel bag with a big box of Irish Roses when Justin blew the horn. Agnes got up and hugged me and she looked as if she might cry. *He's up to something. I know it but don't worry. I won't let him ruin our lives.* When she came back afterwards, Agnes said that she would never forget my treachery sucking up to Justin, helping to settle in Clodagh behind her back and that Bertha said I was going around everywhere as if I was fierce important. *Your treachery is etched on my mind forever. And I wouldn't mind but I never thought he'd ever look for your help when he's got such a low opinion of you.*

9

THE BP sign swung on its pole as they drove away, Agnes's lips in a pointy line, her yellow checked shirt buttoned up to the neck and Justin staring into the wheel. Granddad was glorified as we cut up corned beef and luncheon roll for the cats and took Golly bars and Carrolls No. 1 out to the back yard. We were smoking in the sun and I had my hand on Anne Frank when it came to me through the smoke that someone was roaring *Petrol! Petrol! Petrol! In the name of Jaysus!* I ran round to the front and the roaring man had hair like someone had combed out a sod of turf and his eyes were turf-coloured too with smoulder-ing red bits and he was sucking on a Sweet Afton as if it was the last bit of oxygen. The keys swung madly from petrol cap, sitting on the roof of his coffee-coloured Morris Oxford as I rushed the nozzle into the petrol tank and the pump purred and the black figures on the white screen twisted themselves back to nought. *I could have lifted everything, cigarettes, whiskey, brandy, the whole lot, the whole place robbed!* His cigarette tip glowed above the petrol fumes, I tried to keep my eyes on the black figures. *Will you put ten shillings into her and stop looking at me. Whiskey, brandy, I could have* robbed the whole blooming lot, it would be no trouble to me to put the till under my arm and where would you be then? Hah? I said I'd be in a terrible state. *Oh, a little smart alec, is it? A little chip off the old block?* he spat on his palm and the butt went out with a sizzle. *Please don't light another one,* I had to say it in the Name of Safety but he just popped a new white one between his heathery lips and peppered away at me, *Ye're all the same, every one of ye McConnells, too big for yeer boots with yeer by-the-way big brains and feck all inside of ye but big bags of wind.* He pointed at two dark splashes of petrol on the ground. *Look at what you've done with my ten shillings worth. I've a good mind to throw a match on it now before I leave.* I smelt nothing but petrol as he stood, roaring in my ears. *I saw you round the side lying in among a heap of mangy cats smoking fags, by God your father will hear from me, mind!* And he left me shaking under the BP sign.

10

I WAS watching *Mary Tyler Moore*, with Vodka and Britvic for the shock I was after getting when I saw Justin standing behind me in the mirrors behind the optics. My knees went again but he was only smiling above the gold letters that said Powers Whiskey. *The bus will be below at any minute.* He said there was no one to mind the bar but I was his ambassador and I had to be there and I thought I was going to burst. When Danny Boy stopped for a Choc Ice, Justin dragged him inside the counter. *He said he had to be in Cork by four*, said Justin. *Like he was doing something important. – But he might be*, I said and Justin said that Danny'd only be delighted, honoured to be minding the place. And I knew I shouldn't look at Danny in front of Justin, not even out of the corner of my eye. I thought I would be able to forget all about him. It seemed easy when Clodagh came down the steps of the bus in a Maxi dress, the lemon sunset at Curtains Cross beatifying her brown hair. Now was my chance to talk about Anne Frank and Clodagh's eyes were fixed on my face the whole time. I only half-saw through the window the back of Danny's tractor, a sharp piece of machinery wagging its tail. Danny Boy told Justin he was mad late and I checked my Lassie watch and Justin laughed again, *God almighty what could be so important for that fella in Cork?*

II

AGNES said Clodagh was very nice really. *Very nice.* Agnes was smoking when she said it and the words were lost in a puffy trail of smoke like the path left by a plane in the sky. Agnes said that Bertha said it, too, even though Bertha couldn't stop saying that she couldn't stick it and her stomach was turned and she was afraid Clodagh might be a dumb blonde. Clodagh sat at the bar and her hair was the colour of hazelnuts spreading over her camel-haired coat, smoking Gauloises and smelling of Fidji which came out of a tall beige bottle with writing like chocolate icing across a birthday cake. Sad men who had sat mourning over their Guinness and Murphy's perked up and wanted to sing songs and give long recitations. When Clodagh sang *Here Comes the Sun* in a glassy voice, Agnes broke a tumbler in the sink and cut her finger and they all went *Shh ... Clodagh is singing* when Agnes ran streaming red ribbons of blood to get a Band-Aid and I held up the flap of the counter for her but no one noticed her finger. Agnes was raging afterwards. *When I think of the time I put in here working like a black, listening to their old shite. She can't fill a pint, she doesn't do a tap and they don't even like the Beatles. Maybe they are waiting to see if her voice will break*, I said. — *No, they are waiting to see if Justin will break* Agnes said and the way she said it made a black shiver run down my back.

12

THEY didn't know I was in the bottle shed when they stood outside while Agnes smoked and I was thinking that the way Agnes murmured was the sweetest sound like water running over stones until I heard Bertha say it was another desperate thing about me, going into a state after watching *The Pit and the Pendulum*. She said I'd wet the bed and that was news to me even though I knew I would never forget Maria trapped behind the bars and the puce-coloured dress and slippers walking slowly towards me and the man with the spats and the blade swinging lower and lower and when I ran out of the bar, Justin said I was putting the customers off their pints and Agnes kept murmuring and I couldn't hear what she was saying except it sounded like agreeing and Bertha said we must be the only people in Ireland that weren't allowed to watch *Night Gallery* and it was embarrassing for her at her summer job with the whole Tic Tac factory talking about it.

13

BERTHA said she was going to give Justin an eye opener – he was letting me get away with everything since the shit with Clodagh started. *The fucking watering of the flowers and pretending to be reading the Complete Works of Shakespeare.* Bertha pointed to the wallpaper where I'd written in invisible writing. *I came back into the house, utterly appalled, for I am certain now, as certain as I am that night follows day, that an invisible creature exists beside me which feeds on milk and water, which can touch things, pick them up and move them about, which is therefore endowed with a material nature, imperceptible though it may be to our senses, and which is living like myself beneath my roof. – What kind of shit is this?* Bertha asked Justin and he said *you watch your language in the first place, you are no ornament yourself* and that he was worried about what kind of an impression she was going to make on Clodagh. Bertha flicked back her hair like a savage, Justin winked at me as she read a bit more. *7th August: I had a peaceful night. He drank the water in my carafe but he did not disturb my sleep. I wonder if I am mad. While I was walking along the river bank just now in the blazing sunshine, I was afflicted with doubts such as I have never had before, but detailed well-founded doubts.*

I have seen some madmen in my time. Justin laughed out loud and rattled the change in his pocket, *Leave the girl alone.* And Bertha repeated *I have seen some madmen in my time eh? What do you think of that? Madmen in my time!* I'd written it when Justin locked me in the Black Hole for three hours. She knew that and I knew that but I didn't want to be reminded of the bad old days. *That's not me, that's Maupassant*, I said and Justin went off laughing, *Maupassant by God!* I couldn't get over the fact that I was suddenly cute and Bertha hit me across my head, said I was aiding and abetting him.

14

AGNES told Bertha they had to be nice to Clodagh, it was the only way Justin would see *the enormity* of what he was doing but Bertha didn't agree and what if Clodagh started liking Agnes better than me? I tried reading Clodagh's copy of *Light in August* but I didn't know what the hell was going on and Bertha said *when did this shit start? Explain the story to me, go on! Go on, three simple sentences that's all I'm asking, you see, you can't* and I wrung my hands in anguish. Bertha had twenty-five Barbara Cartlands under her bed. I lay down for the relief of reading them and thinking of Danny Boy even though I wasn't supposed to and Clodagh said Faulkner wasn't easy and she made a big saucepan of toffee and Justin chain-smoked three Hamlets and clicked his fingers and he didn't mention the bailiffs but he said I'd want to go easy on the butter. Clodagh said I was a growing girl and Justin said that there was away too much growing going on. Clodagh stood looking at him, the strings of toffee hardening on the end of her spoon. That night, Bertha and Agnes said they thought he was beginning to crack.

15

CLODAGH and I were eating toast with piles of butter and she was telling stories about the Greeks in the back kitchen and Justin didn't say that I was eating him out of house and home although I was afraid he would. Once I thought I saw them kissing and I had to run into the bathroom and stick my head under the tap. Agnes said I was mad but I said that my head was hot and what did she think about Clodagh's age and Agnes asked me why and I said Mrs Danaher had asked me and she said Mrs Danaher was jealous and I said Mrs Danaher was too old to be jealous and I loved the way she always smelt of Acid Drops and the three white whiskers on her chin like a cat and the way they shivered when she sucked her sweets and she had given me a bag of Bull's Eyes and I loved the frames of her glasses, the way they were the colour of waterfalls and Agnes interrupted to know what had Mrs Danaher said and I said I couldn't remember and Agnes said now was the Time for Loyalty and every family should Stick Together. My heart pounded every time I saw a tractor or smelt diesel but I kept avoiding Danny Boy and once through the window I watched him unwrapping his Bourneville chocolate all alone in the cab of his tractor beside the BP pump. In the evening when Justin and Agnes were roasting mushrooms on the range together and whispering like the bad old days, I remembered that Mrs Danaher said that it was a fright to God to use a young child like that and when they wouldn't stop whispering and laughing, I roared that fact at the two of them like a Minotaur. *It's a fright to God to be using me like that and Clodagh's too young and you're too old.* Justin's brown neck divided into four straining ropes and Agnes had to hold him back while I ran and I locked myself into the bathroom and I asked the mirror, *Has it gone right back to the bad days of old?*

16

MAKE it up with Justin, Agnes said he was listening to his Johnny Cash tapes alone in the dining room and everyone was out to get him. She'd told him it was all Mrs Danaher's fault and *Poor old Justin*, Neily Sheehan had been making smart comments about Clodagh, poking right inside Justin's wounds. It was the Time for Loyalty to poor old Justin so I crept down after hours, stood in the hall with my hand on the cold white embossed wallpaper. Once I'd come down with a cold hot water bottle and they thought I was the Guards knocking, didn't let me in until they had hidden their pints and Justin made a plate of ham sandwiches. How could a crowd of men meeting up to eat a plate of ham sandwiches at two o'clock in the morning fool the Guards? My hand was sliding down the cold door handle as the prisoners cheered in San Quentin and thanks be to God, Justin didn't notice the cream cracker crumbs, which I just saw, stuck to the front of my bri-nylon nightdress. I thought Justin looked a bit like Johnny Cash with his dark looks and great height although Nancy Holland always said Justin was the head off of Gregory Peck but I didn't know him. Justin was smiling and he told me I could have whatever I wanted from the shop but I spent too long trying to choose between an Iceberg or an Aztec so he went off to the bar and came back with a Bloody Mary and I had to drink that instead. It was colder than the devil's hand and my nightdress was stuck to my back with sweat at the same time but I smiled and sipped and he told me about the Overheads and the worries of bringing up a family especially me left so young without a mother. And would I promise him now and look him in the eye when I said it that I wouldn't get friendly with Danny Boy.

17

THE next day I could still hear the ribbon of tape going round in the machine after he turned down Johnny Cash and the things he'd said like the Overheads and that he was as lonely as a priest in a crowd with his worries and I was the only one who appreciated the features installed by Stan Burke the scrap merchant, like the marble fireplace with the black and white tiles with the Greeks holding plates of grapes and the panelling that had come out of an ocean liner wrecked off the coast of East Cork and even the funny things like the railway tracks holding up the kitchen ceiling where Granddad kept his nails. And Clodagh thought that I was great the way I appreciated character in a house and if he was to write his will in the morning he'd want to leave the place to someone who appreciated character in a house and did I know that Danny Boy's father, Old Danny Boy, spent all his time in the John Fitzgerald Kennedy Bar sucking pints and chewing tranquil-lizers and going round in a pink shirt at his age, it was a fucking disgrace and the tape came to the end with a snap when I made my promise.

18

OLD Danny boy suffered from Real Depression, real depression was when you couldn't get out of bed and you had to take tablets for it and Bertha complained about him wearing the pink shirt. Once I looked out the bedroom window and Agnes and Old Danny Boy were lit up by the BP sign, the pump was purring and Agnes was filling his golden Cortina. He was like Danny and the pink shirt just suited him, his black and grey hair sat on the collar. Justin had said that Old Danny Boy's *hair was a bit long for an ould fella* and I said I didn't think he looked that old. Agnes and Justin looked at me and when Bertha threw her eyes to Heaven, they were like blue and white marbles and I carefully watched them go rolling up. That was to stop myself going red, I had a few tricks that I used like that and Agnes said that good looks ran in that family like TB and Justin said he'd met stupid young fellas in his time but Danny Boy took some beating and when we were walking to Mass, Danny passed up in a tractor, wearing a new denim shirt. I stared at the spot of altar candle grease on my desert boot. Bertha said that was another disgrace, working on a Sunday and Agnes said he was a poor thing, he'd no mother.

19

THERE was talk that Clodagh might loan Agnes *Bob Dylan's Greatest Hits, Volume Two* and I was sure that I'd said I liked the Bob Dylan before Agnes said any such thing and then Danny Boy's tractor bounced in over the gravel and his dark hair hung into his eyes and his red check shirt was gone pink from washing and I thought about him having no mother. I hadn't spoken to Danny Boy since I promised, hadn't looked at him no matter how much it was killing me when he had no mother and all I was trying to do was put at him at ease when I said I hated the Master too and how the Master had beaten me over the head when he found me reading Anne Frank under my desk during Irish and I wanted to hear if the Master really had put Danny Boy's head through the blackboard and he couldn't be that stupid could he and I was weak with the smell of diesel and chocolate and tobacco and he nearly put his hand on my hand when I was telling him about the Master and then Justin's sarcastic voice *Can I help you?* snapped like a rubber glove behind my head. He'd snuck down in his Hush Puppies, caught me the very first time I tried to be nice to an orphan. Justin was everywhere, worse than God.

20

JUSTIN is after getting pally with Neily Sheehan, below in the bar, said Bertha when we were eating pineapple bars in the shop. I walked around to see what she was looking at and it was the man with the turf-coloured hair slapping his knee and laughing his head off on top of a stool. *Justin is after making another joke about the Jews.* Bertha had a point in her cheek where the penny bar was sticking out at an angle and I said *But the turf-coloured man hates the whole lot of us, he said he'd a good mind to set fire to the yard* and Bertha said, *Is that the latest, do you think you are one of the Jews now? Is there no end to your self-importance?* I said, *No but the man with the turf-coloured hair* and Bertha butted in. *The man with the turf-coloured hair is Neily Sheehan who owns the John Fitzgerald Kennedy Bar. Jesus, do you know nothing, do you go round with your eyes closed all the time, are you trying to tell me you've never seen Neily Sheehan before.* − *Not before the other day,* I said. − *I find that hard to believe,* said Bertha and she eased another bar out of the glass jar quietly and cracked it in two on the lino. I whispered into her shiny black hair as she knelt on the ground, unwrapping the bar. *He hates us, he told me and he said I was a chip off the old block and a big bag of wind like*

Justin. Bertha came up from behind the counter and peered down at where Neily was nodding away while Justin talked, *He's the opposition of course, he'd love if we all died of a fever.* Bertha handed me one half of the sticky yellow bar and as I put it into my mouth I saw Neily looking at me. He said something to Justin, I couldn't hear his reply but Bertha said it made her sick because she knew that Justin would be praising me to the sky. *He's standing up for you now as long as you're Clodagh's pal.* Bertha smelt beautiful of pineapple and Sunsilk but she laughed like a villain, *How long before your pride goes for a big fucking fall?*

21

BERTHA said it wasn't fair the way Justin made Danny
Boy look like a mope. She'd come to tell me how
Agnes and Clodagh were getting close and she saw
Justin sneaking up on me when I was talking to
Danny Boy again. I piled up too much stuff on the
counter while we were giving out about school and
Danny was saying that the Master was a dirty old
Arab with the stick. And Danny hadn't enough
money and we had to put a load of stuff back, ciga-
rettes and matches and beans and butter and when
Danny was counting out his few pennies, he went red
and scratched his head. Bertha said Justin was doing
it all on purpose to make Danny look stupid, *But he
did look an awful edjit scratching his head like that, you'd
swear he had fleas,* Bertha said, driving a sword into my
side. And Justin said to Danny, *Christ look at your hands,
you'll never scrub that oil off as long as you live now, will
you ever, do you think, with the way it's gone into the cracks
of your hands?* Danny Boy shook his denim shoulders
and said, *No worries as the Aussies say* and Justin showed
off, standing two feet from the wooden till, aiming
and landing all Danny's coppers into their correct
compartments and he said *Au Revoir as the French say.*

When Danny closed the door the shop bell rang and Justin put his face close to mine. I could smell his Hamlet breath and the way he said *keep the fuck away from him* made my eyes sting.

22

AND then Agnes said I had to be nicer to Bertha and I said *What?* And Agnes said that Bertha said I said I was Jew of the family and that I was pure persecuted and I said I never said that at all but that I was talking to Bertha and we were getting on great and she gave me half of her pineapple bar but I had said that it was desperate the way Justin went on about the Jews and that it could be very hurtful for Clodagh when her favourite book was *The Diary of Anne Frank* too. *What if someone tries to kill Justin?* I asked and Agnes asked me was I mad and I said, *Do you remember Bat driving away after his fight with Justin and Bat's face was like the villain Judd from Oklahoma and didn't he drink in the John Fitzgerald Kennedy Bar and what if they all ganged up on Justin?* And Agnes sighed and said it was a pity even though she liked her really that Justin ever met Clodagh, the habitat was upset. That night I dreamt that Judd climbed over the bar and Justin was thrown back against the Powers Whiskey mirror and the splinters of glass went everywhere and one lodged like a lump of ice in my heart.

23

I WAS eating Aztecs with Bertha when we saw all the cars and the vans and the slim boys in the cream parallels sitting on the pump house. *Oh no, Tinkers,* said Bertha. *Are we always to be cursed like this? Justin will go mad if he sees them eating raw black pudding again.* The tinker boys were very dark, I thought they were fierce attractive but Bertha said they looked like Gringos and I said weren't the Gringos the Americans and Bertha was mad to be wrong and she said that they looked like Mexicans anyway and let that be an end to it. And Justin wouldn't let them into the bar even though they came for a bowling tournament and one of the boys was a champion and we all had to say we were going to a funeral if they asked us anything and he called them knackers to their faces and we had to lock the bar and stay inside looking out at them. It made Clodagh cry and she went away on her own to the bedroom and before I went up to see her, Agnes said it broke her heart to say it but she thought Clodagh and Justin were about to split up and I kept thinking of Justin's Hamlet breath as myself and Clodagh admired the nobility of the King of the Tinkers out of Clodagh's window and his big mane of white hair. We said it was all right for the King of the Tinkers to ball up a white paper bag and kick it high in the air. It wasn't litter because the tinkers had a different way of life and Clodagh said they were Noble Savages.

24

WE were still at the window, watching the wind
running through the King's hair when we saw Justin
coming out to serve petrol to Nancy Holland in her
sling backs and I was telling Clodagh how Nancy's
eye shadow always matched her cardigan – blue or
green and we saw Justin say something with a very
nasty look at the King and his companion with the
mutton chop whiskers and Clodagh flinched when
she saw the way Justin wouldn't let Nancy open her
petrol cap with her beautiful raspberry nails and I told
Clodagh that Nancy thought Justin was the image of
Gregory Peck and that Agnes looked like Sophia
Loren and Granddad was the head off The Duke of
Edinburgh. *She sounds like a right gom* said Clodagh and
I knew she must be mad so when Justin left a lighted
Hamlet cigar on the top of the petrol pump, I said,
*wouldn't it be great if it rolled on to the ground and set him
on fire?* Clodagh gave me a look and opened her
mouth as if she was going to say *Run out and save him!*
And I was hoping she wouldn't but then the petrol
was filled and he was locking Nancy's petrol cap and
Nancy was looking up at him as if she had never seen
a tall man before. And I told Clodagh she should go

now before it was too late and I couldn't protect her from the fact that Justin was just like Hitler, an abuser of Jews and tinkers who were the same as Gypsies and then Clodagh said he didn't really mean it and then she burst out that she loved him and it sounded stupid in a Cork accent, like she was talking and sucking a Rolo at the same time.

25

JUSTIN was everywhere and Neily Sheehan was too.
He came beeping for petrol when I was talking to
Danny Boy in the shop and even though I ran out
faster than the wind, his turf-coloured eyes fixed on
Danny driving away and he asked me what age I was
and I said *thirteen* and he said *That fellow you were talk-
ing to looks about nineteen* and I said, *What about it?* And
he said *Are you getting cheeky again?* And I said *No* and
he said *Who is he anyway?* and I didn't want to answer
because I was sure he had to know when Old Danny
Boy was always down at the John Fitzgerald Kennedy
Bar sucking pints and chewing tranquillizers and I was
afraid my voice would squeak with embarrassment if
I said Danny's name so I said, *I think you know his father*
and Neily shook his head and asked me if I could say
his father's name and of course I said *It's Old Danny
Boy* and he said, *What I can't hear you with the noise of
the petrol pump* and I said, *Old Danny Boy* again and
Neily put his hand up to his ear and said, *What in the
name of god are you frightened of child?* And to show him
I wasn't afraid I bellowed *OLD DANNY BOY* so
loud, Justin stuck his head out of the bar window and
Neily drove away with his shoulders shaking. I think

it was laughter and Justin's head stayed cocked at the window for ages looking at me and the BP sign creaked in the wind.

26

JUSTIN said I made him laugh going on about the Jews when they were the ones who invented the scapegoat. *The poor old goat thrown out in the desert*, he said, *with all their ould sins thrown on top of him. You didn't know that with all your smartness, did you?* When Mrs Danaher stopped on the road to give me a spin, I said to Mrs Danaher didn't Hitler persecute the gypsies who were the same as tinkers as well as the Jews and Mrs Danaher said I mustn't make a show of myself crying like that in the middle of the day and she could guarantee me that there wasn't a single Jew or tinker crying for me at that moment in time but she said she would pray for their tormented souls. I thought she meant the anti-Semites but Bertha laughed at me and said I had it the wrong way round, didn't Mrs Danaher know well that the Jews crucified Our Lord? Didn't the priest pray for the souls of the perfidious Jews every Good Friday? We had to look up perfidious because Bertha didn't know what it was apart from that *it had to be bad* and it meant faithless which I said *had to be wrong* because no one had more faith than the Jews.

27

CLODAGH couldn't find *Bob Dylan's Greatest Hits, Volume Two*. I was only relieved that Agnes wouldn't get it. Everything was running away from me, no matter how hard I watered the geraniums and Justin wasn't convinced that I was the only one anymore. I could see it in his eyes and Clodagh put henna in Agnes's hair because she said I was too young for it but I knew it was more than that. Justin wasn't going to need me much longer and Bertha got kinder and said he couldn't be cruel to me in front of Clodagh so it couldn't go back to the bad old days but that I would have to stop talking to Danny Boy and how could anyone be good looking if they were stupid enough to wear cheap suits and identity bracelets to Mass. And I didn't say that I thought the way his straight black hair fell over the collar of that navy suit made him look like a picture of a Choctaw Indian in a casino that I'd seen in *National Geographic*. But I did say, which was true, that Nancy Holland said that Danny Boy looked like Omar Sharif. And Bertha said he did not.

28

BERTHA dyed her hair red and it didn't come out like the packet, Justin said she looked like a tramp and she was a fool to think she could ever look like Agnes who wasn't just beautiful but a lady. *I didn't want fucking henna* roared Bertha and *Right*, said Justin. – *Right, that's it, I'm cutting off your allowance.* – *What allowance?* said Bertha. – *The one I was going to give you before you started this carry on*, said Justin. He held his fist against Bertha's jaw, she was snow white under her rhubarb-coloured hair. I tried to stand between them as Bertha screamed that she would send for the priest. She said that she would report Justin to Father Mulcaire and Justin laughed and lit a Hamlet cigar. *And who would listen to a tramp?* he said and he looked at me as if I was another one and when he went out, Bertha said the balance of power had shifted.

29

IT'S hard to love a man whose legs are bent and paralysed, I was singing that when Justin turned on me, told me to go up to my room and not to come down until I could stop being cheeky. *But it's Kenny Rogers* I said and he said he didn't want to hear it and up there I thought that I didn't want him dead really but if he knew the truth about what happened to Ould Farrell and Mammy, he might be nicer to me. I looked in the brown spotted mirror and held my face against the cold glass until it misted up and I wanted to walk into the mist like it was Wonderland and Agnes said *What are you doing?* And I said, *God, you're worse than Justin jumping out like that* and Agnes said Justin was upset, everyone was down on top of him and he thought I was being derogatory to him singing that song, *But his legs are not bent and paralysed* I said. — *But he's a lot older than Clodagh*, Agnes said and later I stood at the window in the dark while she filled petrol for Danny Boy and he saw me and waved but I stepped back into the shadows because I was giving Justin one more chance.

30

SHIELDING my eyes against the grotto, I crept along the corridor, the silver blue carpet runner lit up by the moon. I was making for Justin's half open door and ready to renounce Danny Boy and all his ways when I heard them talking. *And that weird fucking thing she has with the Jews*, Justin said and I was sick in my stomach and I don't know why because I thought Clodagh would stand up for me. I heard a sound like a smack and a laugh and I had to bend over I was pure sick and the carpet was a tray of needles when I heard Clodagh saying, *Do you know that was the very first thing she asked me when I arrived, do you like the Jews?* And Justin laughed and said, *You must have thought you were in with a right crowd of lunatics* and Clodagh couldn't answer, she was breathing so fast and when I moved my head then I saw four of them in the dressing table mirror, two of him lying on top and two of Clodagh, her hair hanging down over the bed and the vomit came into my mouth. I lay back down on my bed of needles, swallowing. I heard Justin say, *I am sorry, I am sorry* and I hoped he would crush her but Clodagh sprang up from under him with her face shining. *But isn't Agnes just lovely*, Clodagh said.

3 1

MOST deaths happen at four o'clock in the morning. A man with leather patches on his elbows told Justin that once during the bad old days. *Ask any nurse inside in the County*, the man said. *They'll tell you the same thing, it's when the soul leaves the body and some people say it leaves the body at that time every night.* Justin leant his dark head back against the Powers mirror and closed his eyes and I stood there wondering if Justin would die at that hour and maybe he knew what I was thinking because he opened his eyes and looked at me leaning against the wall and said to get out of the bar, that I was an ugly sight and I was bad for business. And the man said, *Justin for the love of Mike!* And I ran to Granddad because I was younger then and Granddad said *Jaysus he's a terror, take no notice of him* but I never could. Take no notice of him.

32

BERTHA said that Justin nearly poisoned Danny Boy with Jeyes air freshener spraying it like DDT and saying there was a terrible smell in the shop. I ran to serve Danny next time to protect him from the insults but a splinter stabbed me in the doorway. The wood under my nail was worse than the Gestapo and Danny took a safety pin off one of the packets on the wall and I had to step out from under the counter and it was like a feather touching my finger when he took it out and he admired my Lassie watch before he kissed me and saw the short tartan skirt with the black polo neck and the black tights that Agnes said looked French and Justin said were a disgrace on a big girl. Danny said he liked women's legs and that scared me because it reminded me of the magician but I thought about it every night and he asked me to come and visit him *when the ould fella was out* and fingers danced across my stomach.

33

IT was too late to turn back. I wore my brown choker that looked like a bootlace, my cheesecloth shirt and sprayed plenty of Clodagh's Fidji. Justin and Clodagh were gone to Cork to see *Ryan's Daughter* and the BP sign creaked after me as I hurried up the road. I could smell the tar and it stuck to my desert boots and the wind whistled in the telegraph wires. I wasn't sure of his house and I came to one with an empty concrete front yard and a van with two wheels. There was a sound like someone beating the grass with a stick or maybe an animal and there was an eerie bird sound on the wind in the wires and I thought of *The Pit and the Pendulum* and the axe swinging lower and lower and I thought what if Old Danny Boy came out and looked at me with his Real Depression and I ran past and Danny Boy ran after me shouting, I knew it was him I recognized his voice but I was afraid to turn round because he'd said he liked women's legs.

34

DANNY Boy said he didn't mind if I was shy and he took my hand and I could smell Lux soap off him and then I heard the sound of a car coming and I pulled away. *There's a car coming!* I said and as I turned around I could see it was coffee-coloured and it was Neily Sheehan and he slowed his car right down to a crawl beside us. *That's right, Neily, take a good look,* Danny said as if we had every right to be there. I said I was worried but Danny just said, *Ah he's only a nosy old Arab* as if that was the end of it. I was so awkward climbing over the first gate, he laughed again and said it was like I had four legs instead of two and then we went through another gate as thin as paper with the rust and Danny touched the waistband of my Levis. I couldn't look at him and he said *do you want to see the pups so then?* And we went into the hay barn. We were under the dusty light from the skylight and he pulled a pup the colour of soot and rust from a tunnel in the hay and I held it and it smelt sweet like Band-Aids and then he put a jet coloured one inside his shirt and it yelped and I said, *Ah leave him go* and Danny said that I had to take it out and he lay back laughing as if there was no such thing as guilt and my hands were shaking as I unbuttoned his blue shirt with his white teeth laughing in his brown face and I could feel there were eyes watching me in disgust somewhere in the hay and it was worse than *The Pit and the Pendulum* because they were Justin's eyes and though he wasn't really there, I had an awful feeling his eyes would never go away.

35

I THOUGHT of Neily Sheehan's car slowing down and the way I could hear a grasshopper so clear in the grass after the car went. It was getting dark now so Danny brought me through the Thin Gate and he had to untie a ravelled piece of rope because I didn't think it would take my weight again. I must have been gone a long time because I looked at my Lassie wristwatch and it was stopped at nine o'clock. I shook it to make it go again but it wouldn't and then the trees began to shake and they scared me and a piece of my hair whipped me in the eye. The ditch looked like it had come alive and I was afraid that a head would pop over the ditch and spin all the way round like in *The Exorcist*.

36

THE big Greek women in the fireplace tiles still held out their plates of grapes. They felt no shame and I wished I could be like them. Danny's eyes weren't blue in the hay barn not even brown, they were black and when he threw back his head, he looked like the handsome devils from Barbara Cartland. *Can't you sleep?* Agnes said, she was doing the lodgment and counting coppers in tidy tubes. Bertha was getting ready to watch *Night Gallery* because Justin was staying with Clodagh in Cork. It was her only chance. The music came from the bar in high bursts. I'd seen that man who presented *Night Gallery* once with his tight lip, like it had been stitched on at a later date. I could hear him now. *We're delighted you could make it this evening because I have something very special on tap* and I shivered and said *Thanks be to God I don't have to watch it on top of all my other troubles. – What troubles?* said Agnes. – *Nothing* I said and Agnes said she was glad it was nothing because she was worn out from carrying the weight of the family. Then Bertha came and said she needed me to watch it with her, there was a DJ all on his own in a radio station and when he played a record, a voice said *Oh Lucifer, the condemned has entered the crucible from which there is no escape.* Bertha said that I could have a Choc Ice dipped in Coke and eat Milky Mints and Scots Clan, one of each in my mouth at the same time.

37

THERE was to be no more about it, Bertha said. I had to watch *Night Gallery* but she allowed me to go up for blankets when the music got loud and Agnes said *Are you mad on a hot August night like tonight?* She was going for a cold bath and I said I wasn't mad, I was cold which was a lie I was boiling but couldn't explain why I had to cover up. I tiptoed into Granddad's room and when I opened the door of the Hot Press, Lucky stuck his nose out of the covers like a gun and Granddad shouted *What's all the tatara? Aren't you better off in bed after the woeful fight below between ould Bertha and that other fella?* He didn't have time to tell me Neily Sheehan was the other fella who was after accusing Bertha of putting detergent in his whiskey because Bertha was roaring at me from the bottom of the stairs to get on with it and Lucky started barking and Granddad moaned, *Jaysus, can't a man have peace!* Bertha'd seen something in *Night Gallery*, she said, so terrible she couldn't tell me, she was like the Pope holding the third secret of Fatima but her nails grazed my wrist. *You'll have to go down to the bar and turn the television off*, she said in a screechy whisper and black shivers ran up and down my back and I begged her *no, no* and she said that I had to and I hadn't seen what she'd seen and I shouted for Agnes outside the bathroom door but the radio was up to the top with *we had joy we had fun we had seasons in the sun.* Bertha pushed me down during the ads and my knees went as someone said *Chocolates no Maltesers?* And the pipes banged as if someone was trying to get out of the men's toilet, they were singing *Carling Black Label light-hearted lager* before everything went black and there was a burst of music and bright light as a man's face filled the screen, his two eyes pierced mine like hot darning needles and he said *The Prince of Darkness has received the condemned.*

38

WE were in the hallway, arguing about the television because Bertha said I should have turned it off anyway, *weren't you there to do it?* I was watching the door handle going down slowly and then Justin was standing in the hallway shouting about fat arses and lazy fuckers and cheap girls. *Weren't you supposed to be in Cork?* Bertha tried to deny his substantiality before he ripped her best green gingham shirt and the peaks of her long collar folded over her bones like wings. *Turn the fucking thing off, turn it off* Justin kept shouting and he dragged and kicked her down to the bar even though she was crying *I'm going, I'm going, I'm going* and I followed after them, wailing like the Jew that I knew I was and when the screen disappeared into a white dot, he turned on me. *Danny Boy the lowest of the fucking low, hand in hand on the road in a see-through blouse. I don't want to hear a word out of you now when I can see through your blouse and Neily Sheehan could see through your blouse. — But it's cheesecloth*, I said. *— I don't care if it's a dishcloth. That bastard parked his Morris Oxford in a ditch, waited all night, deserted his own bar, the John Fitzfuckinggerald Bar so he could look into my face when he told me my own flesh and blood were tramps.*

Bertha was crying but my eyes were heavy like lead and I was wondering what kind of a rat would sit in in his Morris Oxford all night? But most of all I was certain now that I wanted Justin's death.

39

BERTHA said everything was sewn up now with Agnes and Clodagh best friends. Not that she cared if Agnes and Clodagh loved each other so much, they could get married for all she cared, she fucking hated me for the beating was all my fault and everyone looked through the window at Danny Boy waiting on the pump house. And Agnes and Clodagh said I was only saving him from prison, it was against the law and I said *but he doesn't know.* Clodagh and Agnes looked at each other the way they did when Clodagh asked would I mind if Agnes read *Catcher in the Rye* first and Bertha said, *Sure why don't you get him thrown into Cork Jail altogether? If you don't say it to him, Neily Sheehan will do it. Neily said it's his duty and responsibility.* And I got up then because I had to and Justin was watching from the bar. He'd given me until three and the shop bell rang when I went out and there was a crowd of crows picking at an ice cream wafer in the bin and the BP sign was creaking as Danny Boy looked up from under his fringe and I couldn't look at him so I kept my eyes on the crows. He offered me chocolate and blackberries and I ate them all before I explained why a nineteen-year-old might go to prison and Justin's shadow fell across the bar window and I knew his eyes were as hard as blackjacks and I thought if he thought Hitler had the right idea then I was entitled to set fire to him with his own petrol some day and the BP sign creaked and creaked like a horror in the wind.

Also by Martina Evans from Anvil

ᕕ

All Alcoholics Are Charmers

She evokes the pains, fantasies and preoccupations of
an Irish Catholic childhood and youth, with an Irish
tongue for a story and Irish humour . . . The poems
are little dramas and monologues that go straight to
the grudges, disappointments, root-confusions and
hang-ups, showing the depths in trivial things and
the trivial in the deep . . . a pleasure to read and
recommend.

HERBERT LOMAS in *Ambit*

Can Dentists Be Trusted?

. . . funny yet disturbingly precise accounts of her
parents, their sweet shop, recalcitrant cats, school
('filling the inkwells / from the greatest earthenware
pot') and the monologues of Catholic mothers: '. . .
and now Father Tim is all over the tabloids'. These
look like easy, anecdotal poems but they bite.

ALAN BROWNJOHN in *The Sunday Times*

Facing the Public

Martina Evans's poems are a miracle, for the way
they combine total clarity with profundity: the way
the apparently innocent and observant humour of
their narrative surface covers a compassion and
understanding that are often heartbreaking and
heartbroken. Tragedy and cheerfulness are inextri-
cable here. *Facing the Public* is my book of the year.

BERNARD O'DONOGHUE